P9-ANY-070

WELCOME TO THE WORLD OF ANIMALS

Wild Horses

Diane Swanson

Gareth Stevens Publishing
A WORLD ALMANAC EDUCATION GROUP COMPANY

Please visit our web site at: www.garethstevens.com
For a free color catalog describing Gareth Stevens Publishing's list of high-quality books
and multimedia programs, call 1-800-542-2595 (USA) or 1-800-387-3178 (Canada).
Gareth Stevens Publishing's fax: (414) 332-3567.

The publishers acknowledge the support of the Canada Council for the Arts and the Cultural Services
Branch of the Government of British Columbia in making this publication possible.

Library of Congress Cataloging-in-Publication Data

Swanson, Diane, 1944-
    Wild horses / by Diane Swanson.
       p. cm. — (Welcome to the world of animals)
    Includes index.
    Summary: Introduces the physical characteristics, behavior, and habitat of wild or
feral horses.
     ISBN 0-8368-4026-7 (lib. bdg.)
     1. Wild horses—Juvenile literature. [1. Wild horses. 2. Horses.] I. Title.
SF360.S94   2004
599.665'5—dc22   2003061255

This edition first published in 2004 by
Gareth Stevens Publishing
A World Almanac Education Group Company
330 West Olive Street, Suite 100
Milwaukee, WI 53212 USA

This U.S. edition © 2004 by Gareth Stevens, Inc. Original edition © 2002 by Diane Swanson.
First published in 2002 by Whitecap Books, Vancouver. Additional end matter © 2004
by Gareth Stevens, Inc.

Series editor: Betsy Rasmussen
Design: Melissa Valuch
Cover design: Steve Penner

Cover photograph: Darrell Gulin/Dembinsky Photo Assoc.
Photo credits: Darrell Gulin/Dembinsky Photo Assoc. 4, 14, 24; Lynn M. Stone 6, 12, 22, 26, 28;
Dominique Braud/Dembinsky Photo Assoc. 8, 16, 18, 30; Paul Rezendes 10; David A. Ponton
www.firstlight.ca 20

Printed in the United States of America

1 2 3 4 5 6 7 8 9 08 07 06 05 04

Contents

World of Difference

With hooves pounding and tails flying, wild horses gallop across fields and meadows. They look as if they have always run free, but few have. The only truly wild horses in the world today are the little Przewalski's (psha-VAL-skeez) horses of Mongolia. The rest are called "feral," which means they live wild now, but their families did not start off that way.

Thousands of years ago, horses died out in North America. But before they did, some of them traveled across a land bridge to Asia, then on to Europe and Africa. Many were tamed to help people.

Off and running! A wild horse races with the wind.

This young foal is taking life easy, catching a nap on the soft grass.

Most of the wild horses in North America today descended from tame animals that arrived with Spanish explorers about five hundred years ago. Some came later with settlers from other countries, such as France.

A number of these horses escaped or were abandoned, but they learned to survive. They managed through severe weather, adapted to new homes, and found enough food to eat. Over time, this hard life made the horses tougher. They mated with one another, and their young, called foals, were born wild.

Zebras and asses are the closest relatives of horses. The differences among them are few. Horses are usually taller, though. Many stand more than 5 feet (1.5 meters) high at the shoulders. Small horses are sometimes called ponies.

DAWN TO MODERN DAY

Wild horses did not always look like they do today. About sixty million years ago, horses — called dawn horses — were only the size of large hares. Their back feet had three toes and their front feet had four.

Over time, horses grew bigger and their legs became longer. Their toes decreased in number but increased in size. Today, each foot has one broad toe with a thick claw, or hoof, that helps the horses speed across land.

Where in the World

Most continents are home to wild, or feral, horses. In North America, wild horses live mainly in the west, but some have settled on small islands off the Atlantic coast.

Wild horses often gather on open stretches of land. They can survive on rugged grasslands where little rain falls or on sandy islands. Day to day, they are on the move, searching for new or better feeding spots.

Unlike tame horses on ranches or farms, wild horses can have trouble finding shelter from extreme weather. They may gather in canyons to try to escape cold blasts

Wild horses search for food in the western United States.

9

Wild horses live on Assateague Island on the edge of the Atlantic Ocean.

of wind. And before winter, they may grow long, shaggy hair that helps to keep them warm.

In some places, governments have set aside land for wild horses. On the Pryor Mountain Wild Horse Range of Montana, for instance, the horses do not have to compete with tame animals, such as cattle and sheep, for food.

Wherever they are found, wild horses form family groups. These bands, or herds, are usually made up of several females, called mares, and their young, or foals. Each band is headed by a male, called a stallion, that is six or more years old. One of the mares may lead the horses to food, water, and shelter. The stallion follows behind, where he can protect the band from enemies such as wolves.

Wild horses are not nearly as common today as they once were, because there is not as much room for them to roam freely.

NEW HOMES FOR HORSES

Small wild horses, also called ponies, live on Assateague Island, near Virginia and Maryland. Legends say they once survived a shipwreck or were abandoned by farmers. The horses feed on coarse marsh grasses, moss, and poison ivy.

To keep some of the bands from getting too crowded, volunteer firefighters hold a yearly auction. Horses swim to nearby Chincoteague Island, where people buy them to tame for riding. The money raised supports firefighting.

World Full of Food

Eating takes most of the day for a wild horse. It needs 24 to 30 pounds (11 to 14 kilograms) of food every twenty-four hours. Food is not too hard to find during the summer when a horse can munch on grass and the leaves of shrubs. But in winter, a wild horse depends more on twigs and plant roots, which it digs up with its hooves. Near the ocean, it might add a little seaweed to its meals.

Depending on where they live, some wild horses have to work harder than others to get food. They might have to paw through sand dunes or snowdrifts or even

Wild horses spend much of their time grazing.

13

Wading into a pond, thirsty horses stop for a drink.

crack the frozen sea spray that coats grass along cold shores.

Finding enough food for all the members of a band can be tough. Wild horses not only compete with one another for meals but also with other grazers, including rabbits, elk, and pronghorn antelopes.

Given all the time a horse spends eating, it is lucky to be so well equipped for the job. A long flexible neck allows horses to reach the ground while standing. Sharp front teeth can easily slice off big mouthfuls of grass. And thick, ridged cheek teeth handle the wear and tear of thoroughly chewing tough food.

A horse's eyes are also specially designed for mealtimes. They can focus on close objects below eye level, such as grass, while also watching for objects higher up and farther away, such as hungry mountain lions.

QUENCHING THAT THIRST

Wild horses do not need a lot of water. They usually drink just once or twice a day. Where the land is very dry, the horses may stay within about 3 miles (5 kilometers) of a pond or river. That way they can be sure to have a drink when they need one.

Whenever water is scarce, wild horses might only drink every other day. They may have to break through ice or dig through soil to find hidden water.

15

World of Words

Family members communicate with one another. Horses use sound, body language, or both to get their messages across. For instance, if one of the mares in a band strays too far, the stallion tells her to return by arching his neck and shaking his head.

The stallion always stands guard for his band, frequently poking his nose in the air to check for the scent of enemies. If he sniffs danger, he immediately warns the others. Snorting madly, he races, head down, toward the band. The message is clear: "Get away from here!"

A horse raises and lowers its ears to communicate to others.

A horse can say, "I'm mad," with its ears. It flattens them and points them back on its head. If the horse is feeling aggressive, it might also open its mouth, drawing up the corners to show its many large teeth.

A display of teeth can be a friendly greeting, too, but

Curling his lip, a stallion picks up the scent message that a mare is ready to mate.

then the horse would not draw up the corners of its mouth. Its ears would stand straight up, too. It might also nibble the skin near the base of another horse's tail as a way of making the greeting warmer.

If a young male horse wants to avoid a fight with a stallion, it hangs its head low and flattens its ears, holding them sideways. That says, "You are the boss."

Like human families, bands sometimes scold their young for misbehaving. A gentle nip, even a light kick, is horse talk for "Be good!"

SMELL TO TELL

To a stallion, there is no such thing as plain horse manure. It is an important message that reminds others about who is the boss of a band.

When a stallion discovers a pile of manure, he checks it out by sniffing. If he decides the pile was left by another stallion — or two or three others — he adds to it. Laying his scent on top is important to any stallion trying to hold onto his rank. And that beats fighting for it.

New World

Cool nights or early dawns are when wild horses are born in the spring. Mares usually do not mate with their stallion every year, and they normally have only one foal each.

As soon as a mare is ready to give birth, she leaves her band. She does not go far, but she finds a quiet, comfortable spot to receive her foal. She licks it gently and lets it feed on the warm milk from her body. Then she rejoins the family, bringing the newborn with her. The stallion may meet them along the way, quietly prodding them both to head back to the band.

This wild foal has no trouble finding a nutritious meal of milk.

It is surprising how quickly a newborn horse learns to walk and run.

Unlike people, foals can stand and walk when they are less than one hour old. Their long, knobby legs are shaky at first. The foals stumble and teeter from side to side. They fall down, but their mothers nuzzle them, urging them to get up and try walking again.

Within a few days, the foals gain enough strength to run — and run well. If they must, they can keep up with the other horses in their band. That is especially important if an enemy happens to be lurking nearby and the stallion urges the band to escape.

Being part of a band protects the foals in other ways, too. For example, when the weather is stormy, all the horses huddle tightly together. They turn their back ends to chilling winds and heavy rains.

FREE AS THE WIND

Foals born on sandy Sable Island off Canada's east coast can thank children for their home. Hardy wild horses have struggled to survive there for more than 250 years. But in the late 1950s, some people wanted them removed — even used for dog food.

Many children wrote letters to Canada's prime minister, begging him to let the horses be "as free as the wind." Since 1960, Canada has allowed these bands to be free.

23

Changing World

Wild horses do not stay with their bands forever. Young females might wander away on their own and enter other bands. Or they might be chased out by the mares.

A stallion keeps a watchful eye on the young males in his band. When they are two or three years old, he drives them off by acting tough. He presses his ears back flat and exposes a mouthful of teeth. He lowers his head and swings it madly from side to side. Then he lunges at the young horses, nipping them over and over. Each time, he bites a little harder, scaring them out of the band.

Sooner or later, most wild horses leave their parents and join other bands.

When a young stallion starts biting, the battle becomes more serious.

The young horses usually join other males of their age, forming a band with one of them as leader. They travel and eat together until they are old enough to start their own families.

At about age six, a young stallion might challenge an older one for control of a band or some of the mares. There is a lot of bluffing involved. The two males sniff and snort. With curved necks, they prance around, then stomp their hooves and paw the ground. The younger horse might give up unless he senses the older one is weaker. Then the young male would rise up on his back legs and lash out with his sharp front hooves. If that wasn't enough, he would start biting, especially on the neck and front legs.

When an old horse loses his band — and survives — he may live all alone, until he dies at about twenty years of age.

WOW! WILD HORSES!

Here are some of the reasons why horses are so wonderful.

- **A horse does not have to lie down to rest. It can sleep standing up.**

- **To scratch any hard-to-reach itches, a horse can use a stick clutched tightly between its teeth.**

- **The jaws of a horse are strong enough to crush the backbone of a coyote.**

- **A wild horse is so speedy it can outrun most of its enemies.**

27

Fun World

Horseplay means rough, rowdy fun. And that is what wild horses seem to like best.

Of all the members of a band, young foals spend the most time playing, often on their own. They leap around, kicking up their heels and twisting their long-legged bodies in midair.

When two or more foals play together, they snicker, squeal, squeak, and snort. They prance about, then zoom off, racing across an open field. Although there is nothing on their backs, they may buck crazily as if they are trying to shake something off.

Pretending to fight helps foals have fun and prepares them for real fights.

Two wild foals groom each other.

Excitement can trigger horseplay. Another horse or a rabbit bolting past can set a foal off. Even a quiet change, such as sunshine suddenly bursting through a cloud, can start a foal bucking and pawing the air. But now and then, it seems to play just because it is feeling good.

Playing helps wild horses build strong muscles and bones. It also helps them practice important skills. Two females might kick at each other with their back hooves without touching. It is their way of having fun and learning to protect themselves from their enemies.

Young males play as if they are fighting. They even look vicious — trying to bite each other on the face or front legs. All this horsing around will help them compete for mares one day when they are old enough to win and take charge of their own bands.

GROOMING IS GREAT

Just like playing, grooming is something horses enjoy, and it is good for them. Bathing in water or mud helps cool off their bodies, and it gets rid of some of the pests that bite them. So does rolling around on the dirt and grass or rubbing against rocks and trees.

Horses also groom one anothers' backs and necks. Using their teeth, they nibble off dead skin or loose hair — sometimes untangling mats. And the grooming says, "I like you."

Glossary

adapted — changed in order to live in different conditions.

aggressive — showing forceful, bold, or competitive qualities.

bands — groups of animals that live and travel together, like herds.

bluffing — trying to fool or mislead or pretending to challenge another in hopes of controlling a situation.

feral — wild, but once tamed or descended from tame animals.

foals — horses usually under one year of age.

grazers — animals that feed mostly on grass.

hooves — the hard feet of animals such as horses.

manure — the waste, droppings, or excrement of animals.

mares — adult, female horses.

stallion — a male horse capable of breeding.

Index